S0-CVE-691

Snowy Days

by **Trudi Strain Trueit**

Reading Consultant: Nanci R. Vargus, Ed.D.

Picture Words

angel

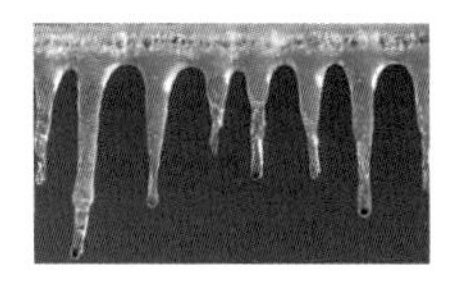

icicles

mittens

skis

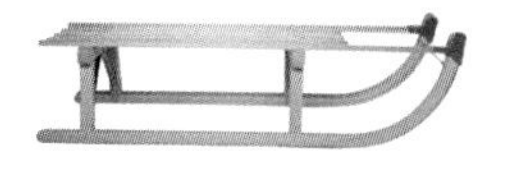

sled

snowball

snowflakes

snowman

When  fall
I like to play!

I make a snow  .

I make a  .

I throw a ▢.

I put on  .

I catch [snowflakes].

I ride a .

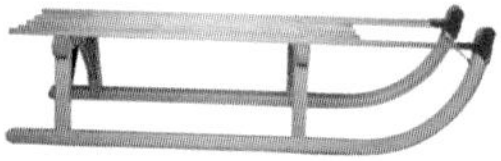

I find 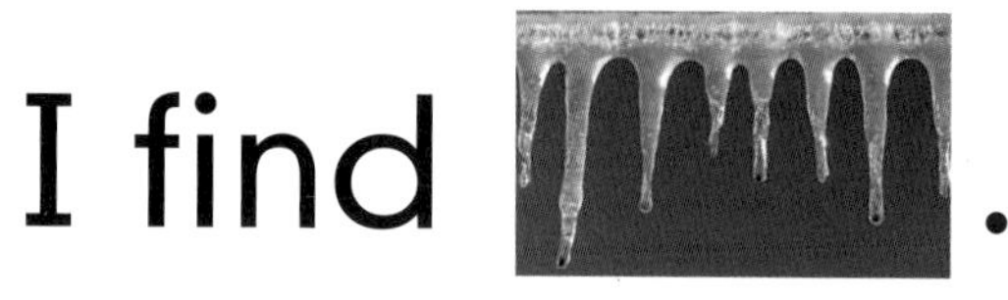 .

Solstice
MICROSHED

I dry my  and
go out again!

Words to Know

catch (kach)

to grab something that is falling

ride

to be carried along

Find Out More

Books

Herriges, Ann. *Snow*. Minneapolis, MN: Bellwether Media, 2006.

Kaner, Etta. *Who Likes the Snow?* Tonawanda, NY: Kids Can Press, 2006.

Rustad, Martha E. *How's the Weather?: Today Is Snowy.* Mankato, MN: Capstone Press, 2006.

DVDs

All About Rain, Snow, Sleet, and Hail, Schlessinger Media.

Snow Day. PBS Home Video.

Web Sites

National Oceanic and Atmospheric Administration (NOAA): Playtime for Kids

www.nws.noaa.gov/om/reachout/kidspage.shtml

Weather Wiz Kids: Winter Storms

www.weatherwizkids.com/winter_storms.htm

About the Author

Trudi Strain Trueit has always loved weather. A former television weather forecaster for KAPP TV in Yakima, WA, and KREM TV in Spokane, WA, Trudi wrote her first book for children on clouds. Since then, she has written more than forty nonfiction titles for kids covering such topics as snow, hail, rain, and storm chasing. Trudi writes fiction, too, and is the author of the popular *Julep O'Toole* series for middle-grade readers. She lives near Seattle, WA, with her husband. She is lucky if it snows just once or twice a year at her house. You can read more about Trudi and her books at **www.truditrueit.com**.

About the Reading Consultant

Nanci R. Vargus, Ed.D., used to teach first grade. Now she works at the University of Indianapolis. Nanci helps young people become teachers. She loves snow! She used to ski, but now she's happy pulling her grandchildren in their sled.

Marshall Cavendish Benchmark
99 White Plains Road
Tarrytown, NY 10591-5502
www.marshallcavendish.us

All Internet addresses were correct at the time of printing.

Library of Congress Cataloging-in-Publication Data
Trueit, Trudi Strain.
Snowy days / by Trudi Strain Trueit.
p. cm. (Benchmark Rebus. Weather watch)
Includes bibliographical references.
Summary: "Easy to read text with rebuses explores fun time activities on a snowy day."—Provided by publisher.
ISBN 978-0-7614-4015-4
1. Snow—Juvenile literature. I. Title.
QC926.37.T78 2010
551.57'84—dc22
2008034608

Editor: Christine Florie
Publisher: Michelle Bisson
Art Director: Anahid Hamparian
Series Designer: Virginia Pope

Photo research by Connie Gardner

Rebus images, with the exception of angel, icicles, skis, and snowball, courtesy of *Dorling Kindersley.*

Cover photo by JLP/Jose Luis Pelaez/zefa/Corbis

The photographs in this book are used by permission and through the courtesy of:
Getty Images: p. 2 CSA Plastock (angel); p. 9 Ariel Skelley; p. 11 Peter Cade; *Superstock:* p. 2 agefotostock (icicles); p. 5 Hemis, fr; p. 16 photononstop; p. 21 Mike Robinson; *PhotoEdit:* p. 2 Cindy Charles (skis); *Corbis:* p. 3 Tom Garcha (snowball); p. 7 Richard Hamilton Smith; p. 15 LWA-Dann Tardiff; *Digital Railroad:* p.13 Bill Stevenson; *Alamy:* p. 19 Mitch Diamond.

Printed in Malaysia

1 3 5 6 4 2